The Spider's Mysterious Friends

Timothy Bates

AuthorHouse™
1663 Liberty Drive
Bloomington, IN 47403
www.authorhouse.com
Phone: 1 (800) 839-8640

Published by AuthorHouse 01/22/2019

ISBN: 978-1-5462-7710-1 (sc)
ISBN: 978-1-5462-7709-5 (hc)
ISBN: 978-1-5462-7708-8 (e)

Library of Congress Control Number: 2019900760

Print information available on the last page.

This book is printed on acid-free paper.

authorHOUSE®

Shaking from the cold and water from the flood caused by the torrential rains of the last couple of weeks,the hairy spider considered his plight as he climbed out of the river onto the bank.

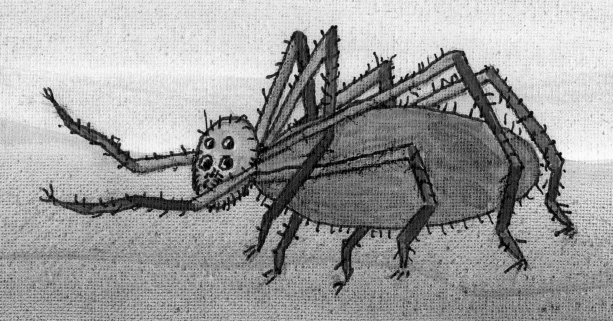

He felt unusually heavy. Which was because he was soaking wet and exhausted from the long time he had been in the water.

Although he was large enough to protect himself in his world, he now found himself in another world with strange surroundings and creatures he had never seen before. Right now he knew that he needed to rest and figure out what his next move would be. And soon fell into a long, deep sleep.

Spiders can go without food for weeks at a time and go into a type of sleep sometimes called suspended animation. Some of them build their webs and have to wait for their prey to come to them while others wander around to look for and capture their food. Which is why our spider could go for long periods of time without food. Our hairy spider was a wanderer which is why he chose the place to sleep that he did.

When he woke up, he saw that the river was lower, and the wet muddy area he had crossed was now grass. The trees and rocks seemed smaller than they were when he fell asleep. Since he was exhausted when he got there, he figured he hadn't paid much attention to his surroundings. He decided to "hole up" for a bit longer while he tried to figure out what had happened and what to do next.

After a few hours he became aware that something seemed to be moving on his back and when he tried to look around to see what it was, he found that he was not able to move at all.

Unsure of what was happening to him, and now he was certain that there was something moving around on his back, and then he heard muffled sounds like voices or a familiar noise some distance away.

He now realized that he was not imagining it. It was other types of insects, some of which had ended up as a meal for him. But how could that be, he could not see anything because of his not being able to move.

After a pause, the still meek voice said, we are at our home. Puzzled, the spider answered back, where is that… where it always is, on top of you…what ever you are…silence…how can that be, the spider asked?

A voice replied, "we came upon this cave with a large object in the middle of it after the flood, and it was dry, so we made our home here and we have been been here for months. We didn't know that you were a living thing."

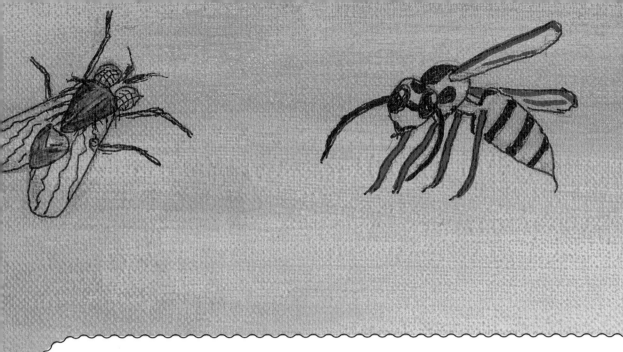

Wait a minute, how can you be so small that you are living on my back and talking to me when you should be a hundred times bigger than you are? Am I talking to you? And are you real?

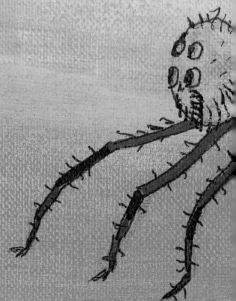

How can any of this be he asked himself out loud? He tried to move but he was still stuck. What is going on? Trying to recreate what he thought happened, he remembered crawling into the cave and while he was asleep something must have happened and he unconsciously released a huge amount of his web making substance which is how he got trapped in here

But that is only how he thought it could have happened to make any sense.
As time went on spider kept conversing with the voices never seeing only feeling them walking around in their world. After several months of this unusual relationship. it suddenly stopped.

Stuck in his prison of self produced spent web fiber he
realized that he could move his legs some, he then tried
moving every thing else and found that everything worked.
He slowly moved to see if it were true and not a dream.

He called out to his mysterious friends... but got no response. Soon spider found that he was able to move completely and was free of his prison and happily walked out into the sunshine.

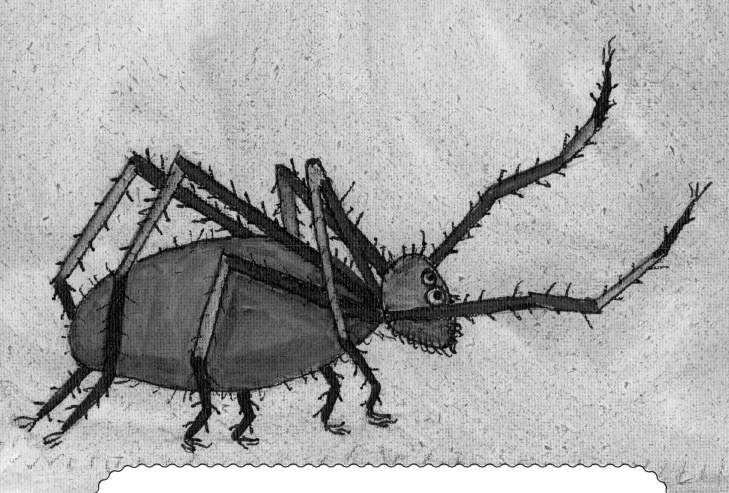

Time passed and while making his way in his new world he remembered the voices and the friends he made and never forgot them even though he didn't know it they were real or not, but he never doubted that they had existed. (if only in his mind)

He found himself talking to them from time to time when he needed a friend to talk to. He never came across the place that he was trapped in again but it was a constant reminder that he would never again question anything unexpected or out of the ordinary that came up except to handle it as ordinary.

THE END

Printed in the United States
By Bookmasters